To my Drewster—May the true spirit of Christmas live on in your heart now and always.
Mama loves you SO MUCH! And to Grammy & Papa—the greatest gifts come with time,
enthusiasm, and lots of love. Thank you for always inspiring me to give! – N B

To the men and women of the Salvation Army – J C

tiger tales
5 River Road, Suite 128, Wilton, CT 06897
Published in the United States 2014
Originally published in Great Britain 2014
by Little Tiger Press
Text copyright © 2014 Nicky Benson
Illustrations copyright © 2014 Jason Cockcroft
ISBN-13: 978-1-58925-188-5
ISBN-10: 1-58925-188-1
Printed in China
LTP/1100/0985/0614

For more insight and activities, visit us at www.tigertalesbooks.com

The Spirit of Christmas

by Nicky Benson

Illustrated by Jason Cockcroft

tiger tales

It was Christmas, Drew's favorite time of year!

He loved the rainbow-colored lights, scrumptious candy canes, and Christmas carols—Fa la la la LA!

But most of all, Drew loved the presents under the family Christmas tree.

There were big presents, and small presents . . .
noisy presents . . .
quiet presents . . .
and presents with enormous shiny bows.
"Do all children get this many presents?" Drew asked.
"Well," said Mama, "Santa always brings each child a
gift, but sometimes families can't give presents, even if
they really want to."

She wrapped Drew in a big bear hug. "What matters **most** this time of year is spreading kindness and Christmas cheer."

Drew thought and thought AND thought about what Mama said.

He thought while putting buttons on his snowman with Daddy.

He thought while helping Mama frost sugar cookies. Drew just couldn't stop thinking about the families with no presents to give.

"I have SO many great toys that boys and girls would love," Drew whispered, "but how can I reach them in time for Christmas?"

Just then, he had an idea . . . a very merry Christmas-y idea!

"SANTA!" Drew cheered. He rushed to his cozy reading corner to write a **very** important letter . . . .

Dear Santa,

My mama told me that some children don't get many presents at Christmas, even if they have been very, very good all year long. I have toys and clothes that I want to share. Would you help me?

Merry Christmas!

Love, Drew

Drew stuffed his letter into an envelope and put an extra stamp on, just to be safe.

The next morning, Drew found a surprise under the Christmas tree—a **big**, **jolly** bag and a letter from the North Pole!

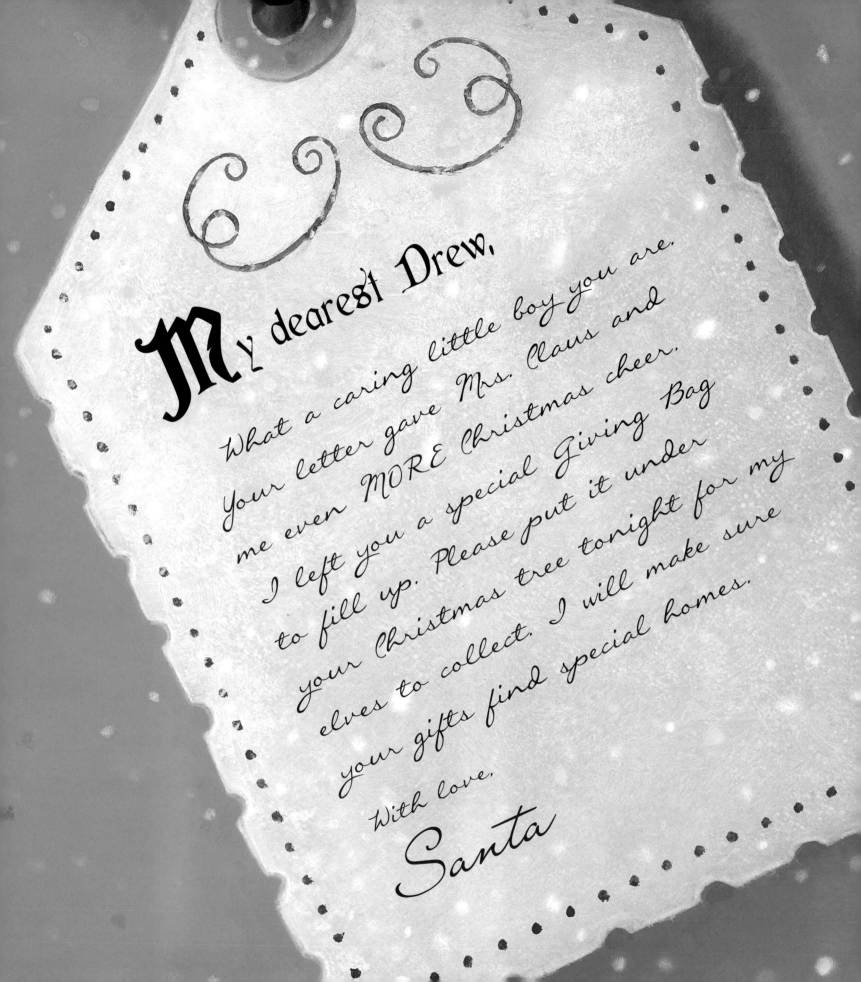

My dearest Drew,

What a caring little boy you are. Your letter gave Mrs. Claus and me even MORE Christmas cheer. I left you a special Giving Bag to fill up. Please put it under your Christmas tree tonight for my elves to collect. I will make sure your gifts find special homes.

With love,

Santa

At once, Drew began to look for things he
knew little boys and girls would LOVE!
He found books and puzzles and games,
toys he no longer played with, mittens that were
too small, and pants that were too short.
He even put in his favorite choo-choo train.

Drew filled the bag to the tippy-top
and tied it with a great big bow.

Later that night, Santa's elves made an extra-special visit! They shimmied down the chimney, scooped up Drew's Giving Bag, and safely put it in Santa's sleigh. Then, with a bright, starry FLASH, off they flew to the North Pole!

"Look at all these **wonderful gifts!**"
the elves cheered back at Santa's Workshop.

Santa peeked inside the Giving Bag.
"What a kind heart little Drew has!"
he chuckled. "Let's get to work!"

The elves buffed out scuffs, polished the toys, and wrapped the presents.

"Now, which children need an extra helping of Christmas cheer this year?" Santa wondered.

He took a look at his long, long list.
"HO HO HO! That's where I'll
G-O-O-O-O-O!"

And with a **twinkle** in his eye and a **chuckle** in his belly, Santa flew off to deliver little Drew's treasures.

On Christmas morning, Drew raced down the stairs.

He rushed past his stocking, past his presents . . . and straight to his Giving Bag.

"It's empty! Santa found good homes for my things!"

Just then, he heard a soft jingle. Drew reached inside and found a shiny, silver bell.

"It's Santa's way of saying thank you!" Drew whispered.

And with that, he raced back upstairs to wake Mama and Daddy, merrily singing—Fa la la la LA!

Now every Christmas, Drew fills his Giving Bag for Santa's elves to collect.

And every year he hangs his special bell on the shimmering Christmas tree.

Each time he hears its jolly jingle, Drew knows that Santa is near and remembers the true meaning of Christmas . . .

kindness to others

and the joy of giving.